Hostage

Published by Accent Press Ltd – 2013

ISBN 9781908917591

Copyright © Emlyn Rees 2013

The Quick Reads project in Wales is an initiative coordinated by the Welsh Books Council and supported by the Welsh Government.

Printed and bound by CPI Group (UK) Ltd, Croydon, CR0 4YY

Cover design by The Design House

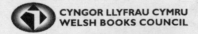

CYNGOR LLYFRAU CYMRU
WELSH BOOKS COUNCIL

Noddir gan
Lywodraeth Cymru
Sponsored by
Welsh Government

Hostage

Emlyn Rees

ACCENT PRESS LTD

Author's Note

The action in this story takes place four years before Danny Shanklin finds himself on the run from 44,000 cops, nine intelligence agencies, and dozens of TV news channels in the full-length novel *Hunted*, which is available now in paperback and as an eBook.

Chapter One

Casper, Wyoming, USA

30th November, 4.50 p.m., North American Mountain Time

Sacrificing someone evil to save the life of someone good had never been a tough choice for Danny Shanklin. Black and white. That was how the world worked. The only choice anyone really had to make was which side they were on.

Shanklin hoped no one would end up dead tonight, but if someone did, his job was to make sure it wasn't his client's wife, Mary Watts. Or himself.

Shanklin was in a taxi, crossing Richards bridge, the arched steel structure which spanned the churning grey guts of the North Platte river. His dark brown eyes stared across the ravine. Old eyes in a young face. Watchful eyes that missed nothing.

Shanklin's stomach growled with hunger. He'd failed to eat lunch. Too busy staring at the phone in his hotel room, willing it to ring. The club sandwich he'd ordered from room service had been so dry by the time he'd taken a bite that it had tasted like Styrofoam. He'd left it on the bedside table, next to an empty packet of painkillers and a half-drunk bottle of Coke.

'Strange place to visit this time of day,' the taxi driver said. 'It'll be dark in half an hour.'

Shanklin didn't answer. Up ahead, the State Veterans' Cemetery loomed into view. Rows of cold white tombstones protruded from the barren ground like teeth. The sun had already set. In less than half an hour, it would be dark.

'You here to pay your respects to the dead?' the driver said, glancing in the rear view mirror at Shanklin's conservative grey business suit.

'Something like that.' Shanklin's voice was gentle, but precise, like a school teacher's. Its accent was East Coast. Well-travelled.

He didn't look at the driver as he spoke. Didn't need to. He'd already made up his mind about him.

The taxi was a black Ford Crown Victoria Sedan. An ex-Police Interceptor, Shanklin reckoned, converted for civilian use. It smelt of fried chicken and root beer. Stuck to the dash was a Polaroid of two teenage girls. A torn strip of tape beside it showed where another photo had been ripped off. The fifty-year-old driver, weighing about two hundred and thirty pounds, had bloodshot eyes from working too many nights. His greying hair was unkempt. Black dirt rimmed his chewed-down nails.

Shanklin already had him down as a family guy. Possibly a retired cop. Recently divorced. Living alone. With alimony to pay.

Not in on the kidnap, in other words. Just someone the kidnappers had plucked from the phone book and told to fetch Shanklin from the Colonial Inn over on College Drive, where Shanklin had been waiting for them to contact him since he'd driven into town last night.

The taxi pulled over into the deserted cemetery lot. The wind howled, buffeting the windows, gently rocking the car like a paper boat on a pond.

Shanklin slowly ran his tongue across his dry lips, like he was tasting the air. An ancient dread was rising inside him. The fear that today might be the day when he didn't make it back. A day that reminded him of the woods where he'd grown up, and where a part of him had many years later been left dead the day his wife and only son had been tortured there and killed.

Sally and Jonathan. Their names opened inside his mind like beautiful butterflies spreading their wings. For a moment, here in the twilight of the cab, in Danny's mind's eye, they flew and Danny wanted to rise up with them, to travel far from here. But most of all he wanted to be near them again.

But then the vision darkened. The wings of the two butterflies crumpled and blackened, like torn strips of newspaper cast onto a fire. And Danny remembered them then as they had been when he had last seen them.

He remembered paper and stone and scissors. He remembered what that animal had done.

The Paper Stone Scissors Killer. That was the name the TV and newspapers had given to the murderer of Danny's wife and son, after the details of the ordeal they'd each suffered before being executed had been released to the police.

He'd made them play the childhood game of 'paper, stone, scissors'. He'd made them play it for their lives, until both of them had lost.

The serial killer had wanted Danny to play too, because he'd wanted to kill him also, but

Danny had escaped. He'd escaped and had saved his daughter, Lexie. He'd not failed her, at least.

Lexie ...

Danny remembered now how she'd watched in open-mouthed horror that grim morning, as he and the Paper Stone Scissors Killer had fought in the woods in the snow. Danny would never forget Lexie's screams and the swirl of fresh snowflakes and the spattering of his blood upon the ground.

And Danny would always remember the killer running. Danny had already disarmed him. He'd taken his pistol from him. He'd aimed at the killer as he'd run off into the woods, becoming a blur, moving so fast that Danny could hardly track him.

A squeeze of the trigger and Danny had watched the killer shift sideways and shudder, but somehow, impossibly, not fall. Danny remembered watching him start running again then, before finally fading into the gathering snow.

But most of all Danny remembered Sally and Jonathan. When his wife and son had needed him most, he had not saved them. He had failed to save them and because of that they had both died.

Again he saw his son, little Jonathan. He saw his eyes shining with fear and disbelief in those final seconds. Again he heard Sally's last, tortured breath.

Danny would never forget.

He would never forgive.

Here in the back of the cab, he cut the memories from his mind. Automatically. Like a computer firewall cut a virus. He threw them back down into the dark pit inside him where he locked away all the bad things that had happened to him.

'It looks pretty cold out there ...' the cab driver said.

'No kidding,' Danny answered.

The skeletal poplar trees which studded the surrounding hillside were flicking back and forth like whips. Hard enough to flay the skin from your back.

Danny took a deep breath, like a kid standing at the side of swimming pool in winter time. He could still change his mind, he knew. He could tell the driver to take him back to the hotel. And from there to the airport. He could quit this life for something safer. It was always an option.

But instead he said nothing. The taxi engine idled.

'You going to need a ride back?' the driver asked.

'No.'

Danny slipped a piece of nicotine gum into his mouth and started to chew. He was here by choice. By compulsion. To be tested once more. To test himself. But he'd been brought here by the needs and fears of other people. Weaker people than him. People he couldn't let down. People who'd paid him to take this risk.

He took the black leather attaché case from the seat beside him and got out and paid.

The icy Wyoming wind cut through his clothes, as he watched the Ford's red tail lights retreat across Richards bridge and follow the curve of Cemetery Road. Round to the right. Back into town.

The vents of Danny's suit jacket flapped like the wings of a bat. The suit wasn't Danny's usual look. The same went for his shirt, shoes and tie. He'd left his own tattered denim jacket hanging in the closet of his hotel room. With a note for Samantha tucked into its pocket. In case he didn't return.

Danny's eyes narrowed as he scanned the darkening scrubland for signs of life. Nothing moved.

Which didn't, of course, mean that no one was there.

With a world-weary shake of his head, Danny took off his clothes and stood naked with his hands in the air. Exactly as the kidnappers had instructed.

Inside the discarded suit jacket was a snakeskin wallet. In the wallet was a set of photo ID, showing Danny's face, someone else's name, and giving his profession as a lawyer with a firm in Washington DC.

Danny's body temperature was plummeting. He'd checked online before he'd left the hotel. Ice storms were forecast. The kind of weather that could kill a man. A buck-naked man even quicker.

He felt like a jerk. No doubt looked like one too. He hadn't even met the kidnappers yet, but already they were infuriating him.

They'd snatched Mary Watts three days ago from the parking lot outside her mother's nursing home in Atlanta, Georgia. No leads. No witnesses. The first indication that she'd gone missing had been when a letter listing the kidnappers' demands had been delivered by an anonymous courier to Ricky Watts's Washington office.

Ricky Watts had made the cover of *Fortune* magazine two years running. A real estate mogul. He'd been happily married to Mary for eight years. Didn't want to get rid of her. Or cash in on her. Danny knew. He'd checked.

The kidnappers had sent Ricky a photo of Mary stripped to her underwear, tied to a toilet with a gag in her mouth.

Every move they'd made had been efficient and ruthless. And Ricky Watts's response to their demands had been the same. He'd followed their instructions to the letter. He'd not involved the police or FBI. He'd agreed to pay ten million dollars in untraceable Venezuelan bearers' bonds. Not even the CIA could track those.

Smartest of all, he'd taken the advice of an ex-military buddy of his and had contacted Danny's new boss, Crane, who'd in turn contacted Danny and asked him to fetch Ricky Watts's wife back alive.

The money Watts was paying Danny for his services would be well spent. Danny's guiding instinct was to protect the bullied, the oppressed and the abused. He wasn't in it for the money. Never had been. Danny was here to make things right, to try and make it up to his wife and his son. He was trying to save other innocent people, because he had failed to save them.

Another cold blast of wind scoured his body. He chewed down harder on his wad of gum. He wished again that he'd eaten before coming here.

Chocolate. If he could have had anything right now, that's what he'd have chosen. He had a weakness for it. The sugar he'd once got from alcohol, he got from candy now. He'd had to stop drinking two years ago. If he'd carried on, he'd have been dead by now.

After Sally and Jonathan's deaths, once Danny had got out of hospital, after the police had failed to catch the Paper Stone Scissors Killer, Danny's whole life had fallen apart.

What had happened in the woods that day … he'd found no way to deal with it. A darkness had fallen on him and paralysed him. He'd been unable to shake it. It had seeped into him, had become a part of him. Time and time again, he'd wished himself dead.

His only glimmer of hope had been Lexie. Like a survivor from a shipwreck, he'd clung to his nine-year-old daughter as if she'd been a raft. As if she'd been the only thing he had left and the only thing that could keep him afloat.

He'd moved with her to California. He'd meant it to be a fresh start. But his drinking and the pills he'd got hooked on had gone with him. Then one day his mother-in-law had arrived from England and told him he was sick. She'd said she wanted to take Lexie back home with her, so that she could take care of her properly there.

And Danny had let her. The one thing he'd cared for, he'd let it be taken from him too. Because even in his boozed-up, drugged-up state, a part of him had known that his dead wife's mother was right. A part of him had known that if he'd kept clinging on to Lexie, then he'd have taken her down with him too.

Here in the cemetery parking lot, Danny flexed his toes. His feet felt like slabs of ice.

Lexie was twelve now and was still in London. Since Danny had got sober, he'd started writing her letters, but she never replied. He'd visited her too, but it had always been awkward. Sometimes she'd look at him as if she didn't know him. Other times she seemed to look through him as if he wasn't even there, or was nothing but the ghost of someone that she used to know.

A good friend of Danny's by the name of Tony Strinatti had died a few months back.

Danny and Tony had met while working for the CIA's Special Activities Division. In his will, Tony had left Danny a houseboat on Regent's Canal in London. It was near where Lexie lived and went to school and Danny was planning on staying there as often as he could.

Lexie was still his hope. A shining beacon. And more than anything now, he wanted her back. He wished he'd never pushed her away.

Concentrate, a voice inside his mind told him. Focus on the present, on what you're doing now, or it might cost you your life.

Danny gazed across the cemetery gravestones once more and wondered whether the kidnappers had made up their minds about him yet. Because if they left him standing here much longer, they were going to need a blowtorch to thaw him out.

Chapter Two

Casper, Wyoming, USA

30th November, 5.09 p.m., North American Mountain Time

Danny stood like the last leaf left on an autumnal branch, shaking in the howling wind. The moon wouldn't be up for another six hours. Patches of starlight glimmered between thickening banks of black cloud. Darkness was closing in.

His jaw kept working, chewing the gum. Each chew represented a passing second. One thousand, one hundred and forty since he'd stepped out of the taxi. Nineteen minutes and counting.

Danny played a game with the numbers. He tried picturing each one that passed through his mind as a different colour. First red, then blue, then orange, then green. Always in that order. It kept him focussed and alert and it stopped his mind from wandering.

Because in a situation like this, when you were waiting for an aggressor to call the shots, the worst thing you could do was to fixate on what might be coming next, or how and when they might finally make their move.

Fretting got you nowhere. It just used up energy. The plain truth was that Danny had no way of knowing how the kidnappers would play this. He'd just have to rely on his reactions and his training when they did.

That and preparation, of course. Because, above all else, Danny believed in the old saying that most battles were either won or lost before they'd even started. And he'd already done everything in his power to get ready for what might happen next.

Keep breathing ... Nice and steady ... In and out, he told himself.

His hands had tightened into fists. The three-quarter stumps of two of his fingers could not be seen. And yet like so many times before when he'd found himself in danger, he swore he could still feel them, even though he'd forever vividly remember the electrifying pain of them being lopped off.

Concentrate ... Keep counting ...

The kidnappers would almost certainly be

locked onto him by now. They'd be watching him through thermal-imagining binoculars. Or a night-sight. From somewhere safe. Embedded. Somewhere they could slip away from easily if they sensed a trap, or didn't like the way Danny looked.

Just count, Danny told himself, trying not to shudder, attempting to block the cold from his mind. Make each colour a number ... First red, then blue, then orange, then green ...

If the kidnappers were watching Danny right now, what they would see was this. Danny Shanklin was five foot ten. Mid-thirties. Slim. With a crooked nose and sharp, angular features, which left him looking more hawkish than handsome. He was clean-shaven and bespectacled. Smooth-skinned. With a tan. His light brown hair was short and neatly cut. A mesh of ancient, childhood scar tissue showed at the back of his neck. Too neat to be accidental.

Normally, his jaw was rough with stubble and the only glasses he needed were shades to protect his eyes from the sun. His hair usually hung down past the nape of his neck and he had to wear a baseball cap just to keep his straggly fringe from getting in his eyes.

Normally, he also kept the scar tissue on the back of his neck hidden by growing his hair over it. Likewise, he preferred to keep the deep pale scar on his right thigh concealed. This was the one the Paper Stone Scissors Killer had given him on the same day he'd torn Danny's family apart.

But Danny had got himself smartened up two days ago. Pimped. Just for them, the kidnappers. So that he now looked exactly like the kind of man they were expecting to deliver their ransom. A smart, big-city lawyer.

Inspecting him now, they might also notice, however, that Danny was surprisingly toned for a desk jockey. Lithe and muscular. In all probability, they'd mark him down as one of those spoilt yuppie types with a personal trainer. Either that, or a fag.

Whichever, Danny looked like he could jog better than punch. Not much of a threat to anyone. Least of all them.

Other aspects of Danny they'd miss entirely. Like the fact that his nose was crooked, not as a result of some genetic kink, but because it had been badly broken twice in the last five years.

And they'd certainly miss the tiny tattoo beneath the heel of his left foot. An intricate depiction of a dragon devouring its own tail, which Danny had inked himself during a temporary incarceration in a Columbian jail in 1994.

Danny kept chewing. Another thirty seconds had passed. Nineteen and a half minutes in total.

Not good news for Mary, he was thinking. Because the longer the kidnappers failed to make contact, the greater the chances of them carrying out their threats. And what they'd informed Ricky Watts they'd do to his wife if their demands weren't met was this:

... film her rape and torture. Shoot her in the stomach. Film her slow death. Post the footage on the internet ...

They'd told Watts to tell his lawyer to check into Room 12 at the Colonial Inn, where a car would then pick him up. The lawyer was to strip off his clothes at whatever location the car dropped him off.

All of which Danny had done. To the letter. He could think of no way they might have yet guessed that he wasn't really a lawyer.

The kidnappers had also specified the exact model of the blast-proof attaché case the bearers' bonds were to be carried in. A Toritech Slim-1. But they'd left no instruction for the case to be opened for inspection.

Which was remarkable, Danny considered, staring down at it now, seeing as how the attaché case was big enough to hold weapons, explosives and tracking devices.

All of which meant, he figured, that what the kidnappers were doing now – making him stand here naked – had nothing to do with checking him for weapons, wires, or GPS.

This was all about manipulation and domination.

Headgames.

Tell the monkey to jump. If it obeyed now, the chances were it would jump again when you told it to later. Humiliating Danny like this was designed to make him easy to control. The same as using female prison guards for male political prisoners and suspected terrorists. The best way to get them to crack was for female guards to strip them and shame them. Embarrass them. Make them feel like children Make them believe they were weak.

These kidnappers were copying this exact same tactic. They were proving to the supposed big city lawyer just how weak he really was. And how out of his depth. So he'd be even more likely to do precisely what they said.

It was a smart tactic. And if their positions had been reversed, Danny might have done exactly the same.

He felt his muscles beginning to spasm. The last time he'd been this cold, he'd been diving in the Norwegian fjords. Training. He'd been ten years younger. Maybe not so mentally resilient, but a little fitter, a little faster, with a metabolism a lot more capable of dealing with a temperature nosedive like this.

Tonight he felt his age. It was almost screaming at him, in fact, that turning forty wasn't so far away, so why the hell wasn't he working somewhere safe behind a desk, like so many other men his age.

Instead he felt brittle and fragile, like the gentlest tap from an ice sculptor's hammer could send fissures zigzagging through him, and explode him into a thousand shards.

Memories of home flashed through his mind. The beach and the heat and the woman waiting for him there. He thought of London, too, and the woman he had met there the last time he'd visited the English capital.

She'd contacted him and had brought him

in as a security consultant, after the attempted kidnapping of one of her more famous clients. Her name was Alice De Luca and she was over six feet tall and had long red hair and fierce green eyes. From the first moment he'd seen her, she'd made Danny think of the warrior queen of the Ancient Britons, Boadicea.

But there was a softness to her, too. The touch of her skin beneath his fingertips. The way she stretched in the morning. The sound of her sigh. And a smile which soothed even his most frightening memories. And which made him forget, if only for a while. He pictured her face through candlelight now. He pictured her face as the freezing wind blew.

Then he remembered where he was. He forced the images from his mind. For self-protection. Because distraction here meant death. Danny lived in two worlds. That one and this. He could never allow the two to mix. Or both would be destroyed.

He forced himself to count. He made each colour a number ... First red, then blue, then orange, then green ...

He bit down on his cheek until he tasted blood. He forced himself to focus on the here and now.

Still no movement nearby.

Nothing.

But as he listened to the roar of the wind, another image surfaced in his mind. This time it was of Mary, the kidnappers' victim. Danny pictured her in the toilet cubicle. With her jaw swollen. Yellow and black. New bruises on old. Eyes screwed up. Not wanting to see.

The numbers Danny was counting seemed to stutter. A controlled anger began to rise in his mind. Whoever had taken that photo deserved to pay.

He kept on chewing, still counting the seconds off at the back of his mind.

Twenty minutes. The clouds had sealed into a solid, seething mass above him. Visibility was down to thirty yards. Danny felt sick with cold. And sick for Mary.

'Don't give up,' he muttered.

The words were meant for her. He knew he never would.

It was time to show the kidnappers more of what they wanted. Let them watch their rich city lawyer cracking up. Tempt them in. He sank to his knees and covered his face, as if he couldn't take any more and was trying to hide his shame.

That was when he heard them. High-pitched engines. Powerful and fast. Cutting through the wind. Rising in volume. Racing out of the darkness towards him from behind.

Chapter Three

Casper, Wyoming, USA

30th November, 5.14 p.m., North American Mountain Time

Danny quickly got back on his feet. He twisted his fingers into fists above his head. He waited.

Four minutes slowly slipped by and still he saw no movement in the gloom. Every few seconds he'd catch another snatch of an engine's growl, as whatever vehicles these were cut back and forth across the hills behind the cemetery.

Always they stayed out of sight, remaining cloaked deep in the dark. They were still a hundred yards or more away, Danny guessed. But were they really getting any closer?

From the high pitch of their engines, he was guessing that they were motorbikes or quad bikes. He couldn't tell which yet. He tracked the snarl of their engines rising and falling on the hissing wind, as if he was trying to tune a crackly radio station on a dial.

Then the pitch rose. Its volume grew. Finally, whoever these riders were, they were closing in.

A burst of heat – of raw energy – ripped through Danny. He forgot his frozen, naked skin.

Danger.

Anger.

Dread.

The hunger to survive.

All these feelings smashed into each other inside Danny, like forks of lightning in a storm. They made him feel what he craved the most. They made him feel alive …

He felt as if he'd just been tipped from a warm bed into an ice-cold plunge pool. Or like a junkie who'd just got his fix from a syringe of heroin which was now racing like molten lava through his veins. Danny's senses sang, as if his whole body was a tuning fork that had just been struck.

He overflowed with purpose and intent.

But most of all, Danny felt like a gambler. He felt like a gambler whose eyes were locked onto the red and black spin of a roulette wheel, as it finally began to slow, and a silver ball clattered across the grooves of the wheel towards where it would finally rest.

Danny felt like a gambler, because deep down he knew that this was exactly what he was each time he took on a job like this. He was a gambler taking a calculated risk with his own life.

He saw the riders now, emerging from the gloom. He grew even more tense as he watched them racing towards him. Two motorbikes. Two slanting silhouettes. Their headlights were switched off. That was why he hadn't been able to see them until now.

They crested the nearest hillside and raced down towards where Danny waited. They rounded the cemetery buildings and bounced down onto the parking lot. They rushed towards Danny like missiles homing in on a target.

Neither bike slowed. In fact, they seemed to be accelerating. A part of Danny wanted to spin away from them and run. But another, trained, part of his mind made him stand his ground. There was no point in running. He'd not get five yards before they chased him down and knocked him to the ground, or ran right over him.

He didn't move an inch. He braced himself. He prayed that his gamble was right and that these people wouldn't just mow him down anyway. He prayed that they still needed him alive.

His gamble paid off. The two bikes skidded to a halt less than six feet away from him. His heart thundered against his chest, as if it was trying to punch clean through the cage of his ribs.

Slow your breathing, Danny commanded himself. Slow your breathing and your adrenaline will slow too ... Save all the energy you can, because chances are this isn't nearly over with ...

There was just enough light left for Danny to make out the details of the two motorbikes. A Kawasaki and a Suzuki. They looked like they'd both been recently stolen. Their licence plates had been snapped off.

Their riders kept on revving their engines. They were deliberately trying to frighten Danny, but they had no idea how much worse he'd seen than this.

Again he pictured his dead wife and son. He pictured the face of the man who had killed them. Danny's fists tightened so hard that he felt his fingers compacting as if they might crack. He threw the image of the Paper Stone Scissors Killer back deep down inside his mind.

Focus on now, he told himself. Only here ... Only now ... Focus on this, or you might wind up dead ... And who will save Mary Watts then?

The bikes edged towards him like a pair of snarling wolves. But still Danny stood his ground.

If they'd wanted him dead or injured, they would have already crushed him. But they hadn't done that, had they? And they wouldn't do now.

Danny focussed on the riders. There might have been only two bikes, but there were three people riding them. Two on the Suzuki on the right. One on the Kawasaki. All were wearing black balaclavas. All of them also had night-vision goggles strapped across their faces. And all were aiming weapons right at Danny Shanklin's head.

He waited to see what they'd do next. Every cell in his body felt suddenly aligned. And trained. And targeted. He felt like a weapons system waiting for someone to hit 'fire'.

Still the riders did not move. Three against one. Danny knew that these were bad odds in any fight. But he wasn't planning on letting it come to that. He was still hoping he wouldn't have to fight at all.

Life was worth more than money. And this meant that the number one rule in any hostage retrieval scenario was that you paid up. You did that and, nine times out of ten, you got the hostage back in one piece.

The bike engines cut. The headlights came on. They dazzled Danny. He shielded his eyes. The wind lulled. No one spoke. Danny knew this moment well. It was the calm before the storm.

The Kawasaki rider kicked his bike up onto its stand and dismounted. From what Danny had been able to make out before the headlights had dazzled him, this guy was skinnier than the other two.

As he stood between Danny and the headlight beam, Danny squinted, and found himself finally able to see. He estimated that the skinny guy was maybe an inch or two taller than him. He was wearing a black jacket, trousers and boots. He had a submachine gun gripped in his fists. Its shape was unmistakable. It was an Uzi Model B.

Danny had reckoned on the kidnappers

packing something more severe than this. He'd been expecting them to be armed with Personal Defence Weapons, like an MP7 or a P90. The kind of weapon that could penetrate body armour. The type used by specialist law enforcement agencies and the military. A weapon that would indicate that the kidnappers were ex-law enforcement or military themselves.

But the Uzi was a catalogue gun. It was something that people could buy online with a credit card and the right kind of fake ID. A street gun. A hood gun. Which meant that the skinny guy now thrusting its barrel towards Danny's chest might be nothing more than a street punk himself.

This was the kidnappers' first mistake. They'd lost their psychological edge. Danny now suspected they weren't professionals at all.

Not, he also understood, that this information would help him if the skinny guy decided to pull the trigger. At this range, the Uzi would leave Danny looking as if he'd just been mown down by a truck. Good for straining vegetables, but not much else.

The skinny guy said nothing.

He just stared.

What was he thinking? Danny wondered. Maybe he was trying to scare him. Maybe he wanted Danny to react. Maybe he wanted him to wet himself or break down and cry and beg for mercy.

Or maybe the skinny guy wanted none of these things. Perhaps he was simply enjoying this moment of holding power over another human being. Perhaps the best part of all this for him was standing here and thinking he was completely in control.

Danny stared back.

He said nothing either.

Why? Because he knew that, just as answering someone else's question with silence was the best way to get that person to talk, so the best way to get the skinny guy to give away clues about his identity was for Danny to do nothing at all.

Danny squinted at the night-vision goggles on the skinny guy's head. He wondered what he was seeing through them right now.

His view of Danny through them would be tinted, making Danny look like he was underwater. Danny's whole body would be tinted a pale and sickly green, like some alien from a badly made film.

Danny would look unreal. Even more so because he was not speaking or moving. He might start to freak the skinny guy out. The skinny guy's confidence might even begin to ebb away.

Or not.

'Open the goddamn case,' the skinny guy snapped. His accent was flat. Deliberately so, Danny guessed. The guy was trying to give away as little as possible about himself.

Danny didn't answer.

'I said open it,' the skinny guy said again.

Again he kept his accent flat, but this time Danny detected a slight quiver in the other man's voice. A sign of nerves? Danny wondered.

Nerves were not something that a man with an Uzi should be feeling when facing an unarmed, naked opponent. Once more Danny found himself considering the possibility that these kidnappers might be much less professional than he had previously thought.

Danny didn't move, still testing the skinny guy, still probing for a weakness.

'Are you deaf?' the skinny guy yelled, losing his cool completely now. He gripped the Uzi tighter in both hands and took a half step forward. The gun's barrel wavered in the cold night air.

31

It wasn't only the fact that he was nervous that the skinny guy had just given away. The guy's accent ... it was New York. Queens, to be exact. Danny would have bet his life on it. He'd grown up in New York himself. His father had been Chief Combatives Instructor at the United States Military Academy. That's where he'd met Danny's half-English, half-Russian mother. She'd been a lecturer in modern languages there.

So now Danny knew where the skinny guy was from. How much more would he give away? Enough for Danny to be able to profile him and even identify him once tonight was over? That was certainly Danny's hope.

But first he had to make sure he survived.

'Do it now,' barked the skinny guy. His head bobbed with agitation as he spoke. 'Do it, dammit, or I'll shoot you damn well dead.'

Chapter Four

Casper, Wyoming, USA

30th November, 5.22 p.m., North American Mountain Time

Only now did Danny Shanklin answer.

'I need to speak to Mary Watts,' he said, unblinking and not stepping back. 'I need to know that she's alive.'

'You what?' the skinny guy shrieked.

His tone of voice said it all. More resistance? More defiance? He clearly couldn't believe what he was hearing. Not after having watched Danny from a distance earlier, as he'd sunk to his knees in apparent misery and weakness and defeat. He tore his goggles down from his face, so they snapped against his throat.

'Shut the hell up!' he shrieked. 'You'll do as you're damn well told!'

He stepped forward, close enough for Danny to finally see his eyes, where the goggles had been pulled away. Blue eyes. Flecked with green. His pupils were dilated like piss-holes in the snow. His lips were bulbous like a trout's. One of his top front teeth was cracked. His whole mouth glistened with spit.

Even seeing Danny staring, the skinny guy made no attempt to conceal the exposed patches of his face. He made no show of regret either, as if he'd either forgotten about the need for disguise, or simply no longer cared. Danny noticed his booted feet shuffling in the dirt.

Drugs, Danny guessed. The skinny guy had to be wired on something. The way he'd started moving, the way he now couldn't seem to stop, or wasn't even aware of it happening, Danny reckoned he was most likely tweaking on crystal meth. Either that or speed or coke.

Whichever. It made no difference. Danny's mind was now made up: this guy was definitely an amateur. And even though Danny knew that to anyone outside his area of business, this probably would have sounded like good news, to Danny it spelled trouble with a capital T.

Because when you were trying to get a hostage back, you were always going to stand a far better chance of success if the kidnappers were professionals. Professionals kept their identities secret. They made sure there was no way in hell they could ever get traced. Meaning that usually they had no problem with releasing a victim alive once they'd got what they wanted. Meaning also that everyone else involved could walk away from the situation in one piece.

Amateurs were the ones who screwed things up. Amateurs like this skinny junkie who was now waving an Uzi up close in Danny Shanklin's face.

'I already told you,' Danny said. 'I need proof of life.'

He said it slowly. He said it clearly. So there could be no mistake. He was here to exchange, not negotiate.

Because that was rule two in any hostage retrieval situation. If the kidnappers started upping their demands at the last minute, then the probability was that they'd never had any intention of returning the hostage alive. And this was even more true when they started demanding the ransom in a live exchange, without first proving that the hostage was alive.

But the skinny guy clearly hadn't read the rulebook. He stepped up to Danny and jabbed the Uzi's barrel so hard and so fast against Danny's face that Danny heard a noise like a snapping stick as his cheekbone fractured, and only afterwards felt the pain.

He gritted his teeth to stop himself shouting out loud. He forced the pain to the back of his mind. He told himself it was heat. He told himself it would pass. He made himself believe that this was true.

'One more word from you and I'll give you proof of death,' the skinny guy said.

Fear. Danny felt it as he stared back into the barrel of that gun and smelt that it had been recently fired. He felt a whole spiderweb of fear, settling on his skin and clinging to him like shrink wrap.

But fear was an old enemy, one he'd learnt how to handle. He didn't – wouldn't – let it govern his actions. Or swamp his thoughts. The way he saw it, you didn't try to overcome fear. You used it. You channelled it into an energy, something vicious and strong, that you could then hold tight inside you like a bomb until you were ready to unleash it on somebody else.

Danny let the fear flow through him and sharpen him like the blade of a knife.

He stepped back and lowered his arms.

'Whatever you say,' he answered the skinny guy. 'You're the boss.'

The skinny guy did a little jump. Buzzing. Reckoning he'd won. He even took his eyes off Danny for a second, to check his two friends had witnessed that he truly was the man.

He then spun back round to face Danny and said, 'Anything in that case apart from them bonds and I'm gonna blow your naked ass clear across that bridge, you understand?'

Danny nodded. He crouched on the ground. He pulled the case towards him. So what had that Uzi been fired at? That was what he was thinking now. Target practice? Or Mary Watts? The way the skinny guy was acting, Danny figured either could be true.

A chill ran through him, colder even than the wind, so cold that he forgot all about the pain in his cheek. Was that why the kidnappers wanted the ransom right now? Was it because they had nothing to trade, because their hostage, Mary Watts, was already dead?

Danny rolled the dual combination locks on the attaché case. He popped the lid. Slowly he turned the case round to face the skinny guy. He saw the flash of triumph in the other man's piercing blue eyes. But above all that, Danny Shanklin saw greed. Because the bonds were all there.

'Step away,' the skinny guy said.

Slowly, Danny did as he was told.

'Bob,' the skinny guy called out, eyes and weapon still locked on Danny. 'Check it's all good.'

Bob?

First, the skinny guy had given away where he was from. Then he'd shown Danny his eyes and cracked tooth. And now he'd given away one of his associates' names.

Danny had hoped the first two were mistakes. But this? He doubted it. It was much more likely, he decided, that the reason they didn't care if Danny could identify them was because they weren't planning on letting him get out of here alive.

Bob clambered off the back of the Suzuki. He was armed with an Uzi too. But the weapon was slung carelessly from his shoulder, the way a school kid might carry a bag. Looking at him, Danny doubted he'd ever fired a gun in life.

Bob was shorter than the skinny guy, but maybe twice as heavy. He fumbled for a pen torch. Dropped it. Cursed. He lifted his night-vision goggles, and jerked his balaclava up to his brow. He didn't seem to care what Danny saw of his face, either.

Danny knew then for sure that they were planning to kill him. He only prayed they'd not already done the same for Mary Watts.

Bob picked up the torch and shone it into the case. Light bounced back at him off the case's shiny metal interior, lighting up his face like a beacon. Like he'd just had his mug shot taken.

Which, in a way, he just had.

Bob was twenty years old, Danny estimated. At the most. He was just a kid. Residual acne patterned his lower jaw. He had unusual tortoiseshell eyes that Danny would be able to pick out in an FBI identity parade at a glance.

Bob looked sick with nerves. Not once had he dared glance Danny's way. Beads of sweat ran down his brow. His hands shook as he took out a paper-testing kit from a bulky body belt. Ultraviolet light strobed, as he ran a bunch of bonds through the noisily chattering machine.

'They're good,' he finally said.

His voice was quavering worse than the skinny's guy's had. He was clearly terrified. His accent was New York too. Brooklyn, Danny guessed. He sounded educated and completely out of his depth. These boys were a long way from home.

'I'm checking the case for trackers and cash degradation systems,' he called out, as he took a second scanner from his belt and ran it over the case.

Trackers? Degradation? Bob knew his stuff. So what did that make him? Danny wondered. Someone who'd worked in banking? Or for a security delivery company? Or maybe just a stupid kid. A student even. Because, as with the paper-testing kit and the night-vision goggles, Danny knew this kind of technology was easy to find online. Or in a surveillance store. Or at a trade fair. Or even on eBay. It was all something a smart undergraduate could get hold of, no sweat.

And the more Danny looked at Bob, and the more he watched his hands tremble and thought of his educated accent, the more Danny was thinking that that was exactly what Bob was. A student. A college boy. Someone who'd most likely been bullied into coming tonight. Someone who wished he was anywhere else but here.

If he'd not been carrying an Uzi, Danny might have been generous with him. He might have assumed that the kidnappers had somehow forced Bob to help them. But the weapon strapped across him meant that he was one of them and every bit as guilty as them.

'All clear,' Bob called out over the wind, which was picking up again now, and coming at them in gusts.

The skinny guy told him, 'Take the case. Get back on the bike.'

Bob clumsily packed up his things and did as he was told. He didn't bother lowering his goggles or balaclava.

Danny said, 'When do I get to see Mary Watts?'

The skinny guy shrugged his gun strap off his shoulder, so he could wield the weapon more freely.

Never a good idea with an Uzi Model B, Danny thought.

'The thing is,' the skinny guy said, stepping up close again now. 'On account of how quick you paid up this time, I'm now figuring I didn't ask your boss for enough ...'

He said 'I'. Implying he was in charge. And that he wasn't working for anyone else.

Which also meant that this was the guy who'd had the bright idea to leave Danny freezing out here buck naked for the last half hour ...

And that this was the same sick guy who'd taken those photos of poor Mary Watts ...

The skinny guy's jaw clenched like he was going to crack the rest of his teeth. His blue eyes glinted as he said, 'Now I'm figuring Mr Watts should maybe pay us the same again...'

And keep on paying, Danny guessed, until they'd milked him dry. And the moment he stopped, Mary was dead. Assuming they hadn't killed her already. Which seemed equally likely to Danny right now.

The skinny guy cocked the gun.

Here we go, Danny thought.

'Get down on your knees, asshole,' the skinny guy said. 'It's time you said your prayers.'

Chapter Five

Casper, Wyoming, USA

30th November, 5.26 p.m., North American Mountain Time

Danny crouched. Didn't kneel. Not like he'd been told. He'd always had a problem with authority, unless it was his own. He kept balanced on his toes instead. A sprinter waiting for the crack of the starting pistol.

The cloud cover shifted. The skinny guy closed in. Stars shone above him like studs on a black leather jacket. His blue eyes glinted like a Hollywood hero's. He gripped the Uzi in both hands. His uneven teeth filled the mouth hole of his balaclava. He grinned.

'Say hi to Jesus for me,' he told Danny. He was power-tripping now. Showboating for his friends.

What Danny had hoped to avoid had now happened. The skinny guy had broken all the rules. He'd left Danny no choice.

'Wait,' Danny called out. He clasped his hands together above his head, like he was pleading for his life. 'Please.' There was panic in his voice. Desperation. 'Don't kill me. I'm begging you. Please. You've got to hear me out.'

The skinny guy kept his finger on the trigger and asked him, 'Why?'

Danny didn't answer. Instead, he slowly separated his hands, so that only his thumbs remained intertwined. He stretched his fingers upwards and outwards, like the spreading wings of a dove.

It was the signal Danny's partner, Spartak Sidarov, had been waiting for.

The driver of the Suzuki was the first to die. He tipped off the bike like a drunk and hit the ground hard. Head first. Neck twisted. Maybe snapped. Not that it mattered either way. The round from Spartak's rifle had already punched a fist-sized hole clean through his skull.

Bob went next. Jerked upwards. Backwards. Like a rodeo cowboy bucked off by a steer. He hit the dirt next to his friend.

Danny didn't know where Spartak was. Across the bridge. Or on it. Keeping to the lip of the ravine. Or flat at the edge of the parking lot.

It made no difference now. Wherever he was, he was in range. Doing what he was paid to do.

Spartak Sidarov was doing what he always did best. He was watching Danny Shanklin's back.

Danny had a real-time GPS tracker secreted beneath a skin swab just below his left knee. Spartak would have been following him remotely ever since the taxi had picked Danny up from the Colonial Inn. He'd have had plenty of time to get in position. And pick his shots.

And the skinny guy had no one to blame but himself. He shouldn't have left Danny Shanklin waiting here so long.

But the kidnapper's biggest mistake had been telling Danny to drop to his knees. They'd given Spartak a clear line of fire.

The skinny guy turned just in time to see the Suzuki toppling over onto Bob's legs. Bob didn't seem to notice. He was too busy writhing, trying to get up, grasping at his chest. Like he was hoping to claw the bullet out.

Spartak had taken Bob down with a body shot. Most likely in case he'd started moving after his friend had been killed. A percentage shot. There'd been too much wind to have risked anything cleaner.

Danny didn't wait to see Bob slam back flat on the ground as a second bullet found its mark.

Instead Danny was already moving, rising, zoning and launching himself hard up into the skinny guy.

He'd agreed with Spartak at their final briefing yesterday morning that if things did go wrong, and if shots did have to be fired, they were going to need at least one of the kidnappers alive. And able to talk. In other words, not shot at at all.

It looked like it was the skinny guy's lucky day: Spartak had decided to let him live.

That said, Danny doubted the skinny guy was feeling too lucky right now, as Danny's skull smashed hard into the bottom of his jaw.

The military had taught Danny how to hurt. Where to hurt. It was something he now did instinctively, like running water seeking out the quickest path.

As the skinny guy swayed, Danny stood upright and punched him fast in the windpipe. He tried snatching the Uzi from him then, wary of it firing. But he was already too late. In his surprise, the skinny guy had already released it. It was spinning through the air.

Danny swept the skinny guy's feet out from

under him and threw him to the ground. Danny went down with him, dropping onto him and gathering him up like a spider would a fly.

Fearing what might happen when the Uzi hit the ground, Danny turned the skinny guy to face it and used his body as a shield.

And Danny was right to be fearful. The second the Uzi landed, it started juddering, chattering out lead. This was why the skinny guy should never have taken it off his shoulder. The Model B was notorious for firing when exposed to sudden shocks.

A terrifying couple of seconds. Then the sound of gunfire cut. The magazine was spent. Or jammed. Danny didn't give a damn which. Only that he hadn't been cut in two.

He flipped the skinny guy onto his back. Splayed him. Pinned him. He went for his throat. And for the pressure point on his collar bone. He squeezed hard. The skinny guy froze. Agonised. His eyes looked like they were about to pop.

Danny checked the skinny guy for injuries. But the Uzi had missed him as well.

Danny was panting. Heat raged through him, even in this terrible cold.

The skinny guy's Uzi was two feet away,

pointing at the Suzuki driver's head. Or what was left of it.

Miraculously, Bob was still alive. In spite of Spartak having shot or winged him twice. Squirming. Making pig noises. But going nowhere fast.

Danny hadn't wanted it to come to this. One dead. One dying. Killing was always the last resort.

He tightened his grip and locked eyes with the skinny guy, like he was locking horns with a bull. Mary was now at even greater risk than she had been before. Danny needed this sorted. And quick.

'I wanted to do this the easy way,' he told the skinny guy. 'I wanted to pay you the money and get Mrs Watts back alive.'

Danny gave the skinny guy a couple of seconds to think about this.

'But now,' Danny continued, 'because of your choices, one of your friends is dead. One of them is dying. And you're gonna be next, unless you tell me exactly what I need to know.'

Danny gave the skinny guy a couple of seconds to think about this, too. The skinny guy didn't answer. Couldn't. He could hardly breathe. All he could move were his eyes. They kept flickering to where Bob was grunting and choking in the dirt. Rattling.

'You're going to tell me everything I want to know,' Danny said. 'You probably think you won't, but you will.'

Danny twisted the skinny guy's head, so he could get a better look at Bob, who'd now started shuddering like he'd just been plugged into a mains electricity socket. Seizure, Danny thought. Or shock. The shuddering stopped.

'You want to end up dead like Bob there?' Danny hissed into the skinny guy's ear.

Whether Bob was actually dead now or just dying was academic. There sure as hell weren't any paramedics on the scene.

No point in radioing for help either, Danny was thinking. Bob wasn't bouncing back from those wounds. Not with the ammo Spartak used.

Danny watched fear and panic flood the skinny guy's eyes. He must have already worked out that Danny wasn't a lawyer. Well, now he sure as hell knew he wasn't a cop either. Because cops didn't just let people die, did they?

Danny momentarily slackened his grip on the skinny guy's throat. Long enough for the skinny guy to wheeze, 'Please ... '

Danny tore the balaclava off the skinny guy. Thin junkie face. Black greasy hair. Tapered sideburns. Face screwed up like a baby starting to wail. The skinny guy was maybe a year older than Bob. Just another dumb kid.

'Good,' Danny said. 'Now you're going to tell me where Mrs Watts is. Who's holding her. And how you're meant to contact them.' Danny glared unblinkingly into the skinny guy's eyes. 'And then you're going to help me get her back.'

Chapter Six

Casper Mountain, Wyoming, USA

30th November, 6.06 p.m., North American Mountain Time

As predicted, the skinny guy had told Danny and Spartak everything they needed to know. Also as predicted, the skinny guy's accent was NYC. Queens. Born and bred. The same as Danny himself. Danny's instincts had been dead on. These guys were amateurs. They'd messed up bad. Now Danny was making them pay.

The skinny guy was now lying flat on his stomach in the back of the stationary black Ford Transit. Hog-tied. Blindfolded. Gagged.

Whatever drugs had earlier pumped him up had now worn off, taking all his bravado with it. He was hurt. The bruising around his face was turning black. His urine glistened on the cold metal floor.

Danny was sitting up front in the driver's

seat, already dressed in black stealth clothing, buckling up a heavy Kevlar vest. The hulking silhouette of Spartak Sidarov was kneeling on the skinny guy's spine, gently rocking.

'So dumb-ass-face,' Spartak was saying, 'you go messing with me, and you are making my day.' Spartak jabbed two claw-like fingers into the backs of the skinny guy's knees. 'First I shoot you here and here. Then when you fall, maybe I shoot you a new asshole also, capiche?'

Spartak was a sucker for 80s Hollywood action movies. In another life, he claimed, he could have been an actor. An Eastwood, Arnie, Vin Diesel or Van Damme. He'd confided in Danny that it was his passion for these movies which had "maken for his English to be so naturalised and off the street" – a revelation which hadn't surprised Danny one bit.

Spartak was six and a half feet tall. With shoulders not quite as wide as a car. Black-eyed and pony-tailed, he loomed over their prisoner like a werewolf – an impression that was only reinforced by his long shovel of a face, which tapered down into a messy and prematurely silvered beard.

The skinny guy squirmed in agony, whimpering like a puppy. Spartak continued to rock. He had no patience for complaining westerners at the best of times. Even less for one who'd just threatened to execute his closest friend.

Danny appreciated the loyalty. And in Spartak's case, he could understand the xenophobia too.

Spartak had been a teenager when the nuclear meltdown had occurred in his home town of Chernobyl in 1986. His father had been a member of the firefighter brigade that had been first on the scene. They thought they'd been called out to deal with a regular electrical fire. But the radiation had killed Spartak's father within the week. Before he'd lost consciousness, he'd told his only son it felt like having the skin slowly clawed from his body by rats.

Spartak had once told Danny that if he'd been a man then, he would have suffocated his father with a pillow to save him from the pain.

He'd also told Danny that when rich and healthy westerners complained about their lot, it made him sick to his core.

Spartak told the skinny guy now: 'Since you make me leave my comfortable apartment with my Playstation and iPad and plasma TV, and bring me instead here to the middle of damn well nowhere, Wyoming, I have been reading from books in my hotel room. This town of Caspar is named for a Lieutenant Caspar Collins. A soldier who fight against a Chief Red Cloud and his army of Lakota warriors.'

Danny glanced back as Spartak continued his lecture. Danny had read a lot of history as a kid. Especially about the Indian wars and frontiersmen and Davy Crockett. He'd used them as an escape. He'd even entertained the idea of becoming an explorer himself when he grew up. But then life had got in the way.

Life and death.

'This soldier Collins was extraordinary brave,' Spartak said. 'He risk his life for friends. But like you, he lose control of situation. His horse, it gallop into heart of Lakota army. This Collins, he last seen alive with horse reins in his teeth, two pistols in his hands, and arrow sticking out from his head ... '

Spartak rubbed thoughtfully at his beard. The skinny guy hyperventilated through his gag. He sounded as if he was going to choke.

'They later find body of Collins like porcupine. Twenty-five arrows shot through him.' Spartak knelt down harder on the skinny guy's spine. The skinny guy's face twisted with pain. 'You screw with me, Yankee,' Spartak said, 'and I will do to you worse. Capiche?'

The skinny guy's scream came out a strangled growl.

Lifting his weight off the skinny guy's back, Spartak took a can of Dr Pepper from on top of his rifle case, and drained its contents in one. He let out a spectacularly long, loud belch, before crushing the can in his fist. The skinny guy grunted as the can bounced off his head.

'OK, Danny,' Spartak said. 'Our new friend here. I educate him so now he comprehend our needs. I think I make a good teacher, no?'

'Sure,' Danny answered. 'I can see any number of Swiss finishing schools queuing up for your services.'

Spartak laughed and made some wisecrack, but Danny was no longer listening. He was staring through a pair of night binoculars out through the Transit's tinted windshield.

A hundred yards farther up the mountain canyon, a Winnebago caravan stood at the centre of a small clearing. The surrounding branches shivered in the wind. But apart from that, nothing moved.

Danny's mind raced. He imagined slipping into the woods. Like a ghost. Through the trees.

He was carving out directions in his mind. Approaches. Ways to get in and out of that Winnebago in one piece.

The engine was overheated from their drive out here. It was too late to call for back up. Or call in the cops. Already too many bodies for that. And time was running out. All thanks to the skinny guy trussed up in the back.

His name was Anthony Arwin. A high school drop-out. A petty thief. Not even part of a gang. His story was he'd followed a girlfriend to Washington DC eighteen months ago. He took a job as a night watchman for the Watts Property Group. Got himself a big crystal meth habit. Bigger gambling debts. Broke up with the girl, but stuck with the job. Until two months ago, when he'd been fired after a wad of petty cash had gone missing from a senior exec's desk drawer.

That was when Anthony Arwin had decided to kidnap Ricky Watts's wife. Partly out of financial necessity. Partly jealousy and revenge. Partly because he could. He'd once overseen the delivery of a home-office set-up to Ricky Watts's opulent Georgetown mansion. After that, deciding when to track down Mary and snatch her had been a cinch.

Arwin was the so-called brains behind the kidnapping. Although, glancing in the rear-view mirror now, Danny guessed he sure as hell wasn't feeling too smart right now. Arwin's dead buddies' names were Bob Harris and Maurice Shapiro.

Shapiro was another meth head. A loser. In it for the buzz and the money. Bob just wanted money. He was Arwin's little cousin. A low-rent hacker who'd run a credit card scam back east. A clever kid, whose learning curve had just flatlined. He'd nearly got himself busted, before he'd hooked up with Arwin. He'd come in on the kidnap, because he'd needed a quick way to raise himself some capital and go legit. And because his cousin Arwin had promised him that no one would get hurt.

Arwin had lied. He'd suckered his cousin in because he'd needed his technical know-how. Arwin hadn't even tried to stop Maurice from hurting Mary Watts. Or prevent Ross Dalio from doing what he'd done to her. Over and over, during the three days since Mary had been grabbed.

Ross Dalio was the only member of the gang who'd done time. Statutory rape. Robbery. The way Danny saw it, this was his third strike. It was time he was taken out.

Dalio was inside the blacked-out Winnebago now. Mary with him. Alive, Arwin had sworn. Mary Watts was still alive. But only so long as Arwin, Shapiro and Bob turned up with the bonds. Which clearly wasn't going to happen. Not now that two of them were dead.

Danny checked his watch. 'Eight minutes,' he said.

'Check,' Spartak agreed.

A no-show from Dalio's accomplices by 6.15 p.m., and Dalio's job was to kill Mary. Then get the hell out. He'd do it too, Arwin swore. For the fun of it. According to Arwin, Ross Dalio was a real psycho. A headcase. So tough he didn't give a damn.

Danny would soon see about that.

'Let's move,' he said.

Spartak opened the Transit's back doors and dragged the skinny guy out feet first. There was a thud and a groan as Arwin hit the wet ground. Spartak tore off Arwin's blindfold, cut his ankles free and jerked him to his feet.

Arwin didn't look so much the Hollywood hero now. More like a little kid next to the massive bulk of his Ukrainian minder. He looked terrified. And why wouldn't he? Spartak prodded his rifle into Arwin's chest.

'I am watching and I am listening,' he said. Calmly. Informatively. Like a computerised message system listing options. 'Cross me,' he said, 'and I will shoot to kill and I will not miss.'

Arwin looked like he wanted to cry. He turned in desperation to Danny, who was now standing beside Spartak, clipping a fresh magazine into his MK 23 pistol.

'Please,' Arwin said, his voice now quavering like he was speeding over bumps in a car. 'Ross sees me turn up on my own and he'll do her. I swear it. He'll know we've screwed up. He'll do me and then he'll do the bitch.'

Bitch ... it took all of Danny's self-control not to knock him right back to the ground again.

'You let me worry about that,' Danny said. 'You just keep him talking.'

'And think about the barrel of this gun pointing at the back of your head,' Spartak said. 'Do not try and be brave like a cowboy, Yankee. Do not end up dead like that Lieutenant Collins or your John Wayne.'

Danny stared into the cold, dark woods. There were many places he'd rather be. But his work was here. And so was Mary. It was time to finish what Anthony Arwin had begun.

'Give me a one minute start,' Danny told his friend. 'Then cut him loose.'

Chapter Seven

Casper Mountain, Wyoming, USA

30th November, 6.09 p.m., North American Mountain Time

The icy wind hissed like static in the trees. The air was heavy with moisture and the dank scent of pine. Danny ran due south to begin with. Away from the Winnebago. Into the undergrowth. Balaclava down. Night-vision goggles on.

The goggles fed off light thrown down from the stars and the faint miasma cast up from the nearby city of Casper. They were auto-focussing. Retina-guided. Smart-chipped. A world away from the spy-shop crap Arwin and his team had been tooled up with.

The goggles turned Danny's vision night-green but crystal clear also. As if he was lancing through stagnant water, a ravenous pike in search of prey.

The thermal-imaging sub-programme in the goggles showed up rabbits and mule deer as patches of red. But Danny saw nothing any bigger than these. Certainly no people. And Danny was lucky in this at least. Because there could have been campers up here. Hunters too, here to kill pronghorn and elk. He had the weather to thank for the fact that there weren't.

As he ran across the wet ground, Danny hardly made a sound. He was in his element now. Even before he'd joined the military, his father had taught him how to hunt at night.

After a hundred yards, Danny began his loop. First round to the west. Then north. Hurdling fallen branches. Weaving through the bushes and trees. Until the long rectangular silhouette of the Winnebago finally came back into sight. This time from the rear.

Danny slowed. Thirty yards out now. Moving in.

Arwin had told him that Ross Dalio was the only one in there. But Danny only ever believed what he saw with his own eyes. He scanned the ground around the back of the Winnebago. Plenty of bootprints. Could be those of Arwin and the dead guys. Or maybe there were more of them inside.

There was a single door at the back of the Winnebago. A crack of light showed. Which meant the door was either loose or unlocked. Two windows. Blinds down. Danny's goggles showed a patch of fierce red to the right of the door. Most likely a stove. A lighter patch to the left. Down low.

Could be someone slumped in a confined space against the back wall. Danny was guessing Mary. Just like in the photo. In the toilet. Limbs bunched up. Most likely gagged and tied. Or drugged.

Danny ditched his goggles. Dalio had the lights on inside. Bust in there with his goggles on and he would be left blind.

He checked the luminous hands on his watch. Three minutes left till Dalio was due to execute Mary and clear out.

Spartak would be out there in the woods just like Danny. Both of them settling into position. Moving with precision. Like two lethal dancers.

Danny moved in closer to the Winnebago. He waited with his back pressed close against a tree.

He didn't need to worry about Spartak. If anything, the Ukrainian was better trained than Danny himself. Ex-KGB and FSB. But like Danny he was a freelancer now. He wasn't afraid of anything except drowning. And the nearest deep river was three kilometres away.

Danny trusted Spartak Sidarov with his life.

Arwin's voice broke the silence of the cool night air. Round the front of the Winnebago. Beyond Danny's line of sight.

'Ross,' he called out. 'It's me, Tony.'

Silence, then:

'What about the others?' another man called back.

Ross Dalio. The rapist. The one who'd been taking his time with Mary. Again, Danny pictured the bruises on her face and neck. He nodded to himself. Not long now, before the two of them met.

'They're back down the trail,' Arwin yelled back. 'We blew a tyre. So come on out here. We're gonna need your help.'

So far, so good, Danny was thinking. Arwin was doing what he'd been told, drawing his accomplice out.

But then Dalio shouted. 'Where's your bike?'

'Back there in the trees.'

'I never heard you coming.'

Arwin didn't answer.

Dalio called out, 'Come out where I can see

you.' There was a pause. 'Do it, or I ain't coming out at all.'

'OK, man. OK.'

Another pause, then Dalio's voice exploded with fury. 'What the fuck?' he shouted. 'What the fuck is wrong with your face?'

The bruising. Dalio must have spotted it, even in the dark.

Danny moved quickly. Up to the Winnebago, beneath the window. Using a palm mirror, he searched the curtain for a gap, a way to see in. But he couldn't even get a glimpse.

Out front, Arwin shrieked. 'No. Don't. It's not what you think. It's ...'

Then Danny heard what he'd hoped he wouldn't.

A shotgun roared. Once. Twice. It echoed through the night. Its retort sounded like a double barrel to Danny. This wasn't the kind of thing he'd normally bet his life on, but tonight he had no choice.

Arwin was most likely already dead. Mary would be next. The time for caution had gone.

Danny drew his pistol and busted shoulder-first through the back door of the Winnebago.

He scrambled inside. Sprawled. But then his pistol flew from his grip and skittered across the laminate floor. He had been snagged by a tripwire. This Dalio clearly wasn't as dumb as his friends.

But fortunately he wasn't a genius either.

Black-bearded, long-haired, with tattoos running the lengths of his arms – Dalio was crouched by the front door. As he spun round to face Danny, Danny saw that he'd been right: the shotgun Dalio was holding was a Benelli. Double barrelled, not pump.

Dalio swung round, aimed at Danny, and pulled the trigger. But all the gun did was click. As Danny scrabbled to his feet and dived for his pistol, Dalio did the math that Danny'd already done. Two shots fired. No shots left. He leapt to his feet and raised the gun like a club above his head. Then brought it swinging down.

Danny rolled left, crashing into the table. A fold-out. The surface went from ninety degrees right through to one-eighty. It slammed Danny down hard against the wall. Plastic plates and steel pans clattered to the floor. Danny lunged for his pistol. But Dalio got there first. He kicked it spinning away. Under the stove. Out of reach.

Dalio roared, swung again. Again Danny rolled. Again he escaped the blow. This time, Dalio's momentum carried him on past Danny.

He teetered in the open back doorway. Danny didn't hesitate. He kicked out and sent him tumbling into the night.

Danny was on him in less than two seconds.

Dalio was strong, stronger than Danny. But Danny was better trained. He took him round the throat. Cut off his oxygen supply. Cut off his strength. The bigger man made a high-pitched keening sound as Danny upped the pressure. Only a matter of time now until he passed out.

But Dalio still wouldn't quit. He kept flapping his arms around, trying to pull Danny off.

Then Danny heard a schnicking noise. Metal on metal. The unmistakable sound of a stiletto knife being drawn.

Danny didn't try to disarm him. Too big a risk. He couldn't even know which hand the knife was in. He did the only thing he could to ensure his and Mary's safety. He quit trying to pacify Dalio. He decided to kill him instead.

He did it quick. Like he'd been taught to. Cranked the neck. Whipped the chin sideways. Forced the crown down hard the opposite way. Dalio's body spasmed. Then went slack.

Danny tightened his grip on Dalio's neck,

just to be sure. He clamped Dalio's head tight against his chest. Then stared into his eyes. Dalio's pupils dilated in the rectangle of light thrown down from the open Winnebago door. It was the last movement they made.

A creaking sound. A shadow fell. Danny twisted round to see Spartak standing in the open doorway.

'Clear,' he said. He must have broken in the other side.

'How is she?' Danny asked. She. Mary. The reason they were here.

'Alive. Handcuffed. She will not speak to me.'

'What about Arwin?'

'Roadkill. And that guy?'

'The same.'

Danny turned Dalio's corpse over and went through his pockets. He found a golden Zippo lighter engraved with Dalio's initials. A tobacco pouch and two twenty-dollar bills. Then what Danny had been looking for: keys for the cuffs.

He stood. He slipped Dalio's Zippo into his pocket.

'Call Crane,' he said. 'Tell him it's done. Tell him how many bodies he's going to have to make disappear.'

Four dead. And Danny didn't give a damn

about any of them, except for maybe Bob. Camp follower. Most likely bullied and coerced. As for the rest of Arwin's crew, they'd got what they deserved. Never start a fight you can't finish. They should have thought about that, before they'd decided to destroy Mary's life.

It wouldn't take Crane long to get here. He was only a few miles away, waiting for news with Ricky Watts. He had a clean-up team with him. The fact that there were no survivors meant a lot less hassle for everyone involved. It meant there was no need to involve the police. All they needed to do was dispose of the bodies. The Winnebago would be burned. It would be like none of this had happened.

Except for Mary. For her the last three days might never end.

Danny went back inside to tend to her. He noticed the smells now. Cheap cigarettes. Spilt beer. Pizza. He pulled a blanket off one of the bunks as he passed.

He found Mary in the toilet cubicle. Bruised. Filthy. Her eyes were glazed. She stared through him as he knelt down beside her and gently covered her with the blanket.

'You're safe now,' he said as he took off her restraints. 'It's over.' Her wrists were black and bloody. Three of her fingers were broken. He was still full of adrenaline, but he forced his voice to be calm. 'I work for your husband,' he said. 'He sent me to find you. I'm here to take you home.'

Her eyes registered nothing. She didn't even blink. Danny checked her pulse. It was regular. She might have been at home watching TV. It was obvious to him that something inside her had switched off. Had been snapped.

'You need to come with me now,' he said, slipping his hands beneath her arms and raising her up.

She didn't resist. Didn't do anything. Didn't even try to support herself. He lifted her out of the cubicle and up onto him, her chin resting on his shoulder, looking back. She didn't move. She was dead weight. A casualty.

But when he walked towards the open front door through which Spartak had entered, her body went rigid. It was as if she'd been electrocuted. Then she started screaming. She tore herself free.

Danny looked back and saw Dalio. Raised up high the way she'd been, Mary had seen his body behind them. Out through the open back door. Lying there in the dirt.

Now she ran at it and threw herself upon it. She started screeching, cursing, beating it, clawing, ripping at Dalio's warm dead flesh with her jagged nails and teeth.

Danny didn't try to stop her. He understood. He looked away and waited for her to burn herself out.

He went to her then. He wrapped the blanket around her once more and held her in his arms. Mucus encrusted her lips. Her eyes were slits. Her breathing slowed. Within seconds, he knew, she'd be asleep.

'Can you hear me, Mary?'

When she didn't respond at the second time of asking, he lifted her onto his shoulder and walked with her into the dark. He'd carry her to the Transit. Into the warmth. He'd keep her safe until her husband came to take her away.

Quick Reads 📖

Books in the Quick Reads series